For Mom and Dad,
for always encouraging me
to find my own path

—M.S.

All rights reserved. Published in the United States by Random House Studio,
an imprint of Random House Children's Books, a division of Penguin Random House LLC, New York.

Random House Studio with colophon is a registered trademark of Penguin Random House LLC.

Visit us on the Web! rhcbooks.com

Educators and librarians, for a variety of teaching tools, visit us at
RHTeachersLibrarians.com

Library of Congress Cataloging-in-Publication Data is available upon request.
ISBN 978-0-593-64827-8 (trade) — ISBN 978-0-593-64828-5 (lib. bdg.) —
ISBN 978-0-593-64829-2 (ebook)

The artist used paint and paper textures combined with digital media
to create the illustrations for this book.
The text of this book is set in 16-point Milo Serif Medium.
Interior design by Rachael Cole and Paula Baver

MANUFACTURED IN CHINA
10 9 8 7 6 5 4 3 2 1
First Edition

FRASER
THE FOREST RANGER

MATTHEW SCHUFMAN

RANDOM HOUSE STUDIO ⌂ NEW YORK

Fraser loved the forest.
He watched over it from his
cabin on top of Pine Peak.

Each morning, he would walk
down from his hill and check on
the trees and animals.

Each night, he would walk back up, make a large
stack of pancakes for dinner, and rest by the fire.

Although Fraser loved being a ranger, he did everything alone.

He played games alone.

Paddled alone.

Danced alone.

He even celebrated his birthday alone.

Being alone all the time was okay, but Fraser thought it might be nice to meet someone new.

So the next morning, Fraser set out to see if he could find a friend.

After walking for some time, Fraser came
upon a large lake. Crowds of people were lying
on the beach. People were playing volleyball.
Boats bobbed on the water.

The hot sun beat down on Fraser.
I miss the cool shade of the trees.
This isn't the place for me, he thought.

Fraser kept walking and found a busy zoo.

People bustled around with hot dogs and balloons. Although the people were smiling, Fraser couldn't help but notice that all the animals looked sad.

I miss my animal friends, thought Fraser. He decided to keep searching.

Fraser walked for miles and miles and
eventually came upon a large city.

"I must be very far from home. There are a lot of people in cities. I'm sure I'll be able to find a friend here."

Fraser stood on a very busy street for hours and greeted everyone who passed by.

Some people brushed past him. Some listened to music. Some talked on phones. No one stopped to talk.

Fraser sat on a city bench, defeated. The lights in the buildings were so bright he couldn't see any stars, as he could back home.

I miss the trees and stars, thought Fraser. It's time for me to go back home to the forest, where I belong.

By the time Fraser reached the forest, it was very late.

The trails were dark and hard to see.

Finally, he climbed
the hill to his cabin.

Fraser opened the door and gasped.
There was a stranger in his cabin!
"I'm Fraser. What are you doing in
my cabin?" he asked.

"I'm Hazel. What are you doing in MY cabin?" she replied. "This is the Maple Ridge Ranger Station. Are you sure you're in the right place?" she asked.

"I'm so sorry to bother you," said Fraser
as he left the cabin. "I must've taken a wrong
turn in the dark. I'll be on my way...."

"Wait!" said Hazel. "Why don't you
stay for dinner? I just made pancakes!"

The two new friends stayed up late eating pancakes

and sharing stories about the forest.

Fraser loved the forest. His favorite part was having a friend close by.